MARY POPPINS
IN CHERRY TREE LANE

The Mary Poppins Books

MARY POPPINS
MARY POPPINS COMES BACK
MARY POPPINS OPENS THE DOOR
MARY POPPINS IN THE PARK
MARY POPPINS IN THE KITCHEN

William Collins Sons & Co Ltd
London · Glasgow · Sydney · Auckland
Toronto · Johannesburg

First published 1982
© Text P. L. Travers 1982
© Illustrations Mary Shepard 1982
ISBN 0 00 181112 6

Made and printed in Great Britain by
William Collins Sons & Co Ltd Glasgow

Mary Poppins in Cherry Tree Lane

P. L. TRAVERS

with illustrations by
MARY SHEPARD

COLLINS

To
K. L. T.
and
C. J. T

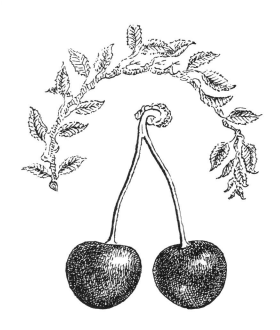

It was Midsummer's Eve. This is the most magical night of the year. Many curious things can happen in it before it gives way to the dawn. But it was not night yet by any means. The sun, still bright, was dawdling to the west, lazily taking his time about it, as though reluctant to leave the world.

He felt that he had done it proud, putting upon it a shine and a polish that would not quickly fade. His own reflection shone back at him from fountains, lakes and window-panes, even from the ripened fruit that hung in the trees of Cherry Tree Lane, a place well known to him.

9

"Nothing like sunshine," he flattered himself, as he noted the glitter of the ship's lanterns on either side of the Admiral's gate; the sparkle of the brass knocker on the door of Miss Lark's mansion; the gleam that came from an old tin toy, abandoned, apparently, by its owners, in the garden of the smallest house. This, too, was a place well known to him.

"Not a soul in sight," he thought to himself, as he sent his long light over the Lane and then across the open space, large and green and blossoming, that spread beside and beyond it. And this, too, he knew well. After all, he had had a hand in its making. For where would they be – tree, grass and flower – without, as it were, his helping hand, greening the grass, coaxing the leaf from the bare bough, warming the bud into flower?

And here, among lengthening light and shadows, there *was* a soul in sight.

"Who's that, down there in the Park?" he wondered, as a curious figure went back and forth, blowing a whistle and shouting.

Who else could it be but the Park Keeper? It was no wonder, however, that the sun did not recognize him for, in spite of the heavy heat of June, he was wearing a black, felt, sea-faring hat painted with skull-and-crossbones.

"Obey the rules! Remember the bye-laws! All

litter to be placed in the baskets!" he bellowed.

But nobody took any notice. People went strolling hand in hand; scattering litter as they went; deliberately sauntering on lawns whose notices said KEEP OFF THE GRASS; failing to observe the rules; forgetting all the bye-laws.

The Policeman was marching to and fro, swinging his baton and looking important, as if he thought he owned the earth and expected the earth to be glad of it.

Children went up and down on the swings, swooping like evening swallows.

And the swallows sang their songs so loudly that nobody heard the Park Keeper's whistle.

Admiral and Mrs Boom, sharing a bag of peanuts between them and dropping the empty shells as they went, were taking the air in the Long Walk.

"Oh, I'm roaming
In the gloaming
With my lassie by my side!"

sang the Admiral, disregarding the signboard's warning NO HAWKERS, NO MUSICIANS.

In the Rose Garden, a tall man, in a cricketing cap a little too small and skimpy for him, was dipping his handkerchief into the fountain and was mopping his sunburnt brow.

Down by the Lake, an elderly gentleman in a hat of folded newpaper stood turning his head this way and that, sniffing the air like a gun dog.

"Coo-ee, Professor!" called Miss Lark, hurrying across the lawns, with her dogs unwillingly dragging behind her, as though they wished they were somewhere else.

For Miss Lark, to celebrate Midsummer's Eve, had tied a ribbon upon each head – pink for Willoughby, blue for Andrew – and they felt ashamed and dejected. What, they wondered, would people think? They might be mistaken for poodles!

"Professor, I've been waiting for you. You must have lost your way."

"Well, that's the way with ways, I suppose. Either you lose them or they lose you. Anyway, you've found me, Miss Sparrow. But alas!" he fanned himself with his hat, "I find the Sahara Desert a little – um – er – hot."

"You are not in the Sahara, Professor. You are in the Park. Don't you remember? I invited you to supper."

"Ah, so you did. To Strawberry Street. I hope it will be cooler there. For you and me and your two – um – poodles."

Andrew and Willoughby hung their heads. Their

worst fears had been realized.

"No, no. The address is Cherry Tree Lane. And my name is Lucinda Lark. Do try not to be so forgetful. Ah, there you are, dear friends!" she trilled, as she spied the Booms in the distance. "Where are you off to this beautiful evening?"

"Sailing, sailing, over the bounding main," sang the Admiral. "And many a stormy wind shall blow, till Jack comes home again – won't it, Messmate?" he enquired of his wife.

"Yes, dear," murmured Mrs. Boom. "Unless you would like to wait till tomorrow. Binnacle is making Cottage Pie and there will be Apple Tart for dinner."

"Cottage Pie! I can't miss that. Let down the anchor, Midshipman. We'll wait for the morning tide."

"Yes, dear," Mrs Boom agreed. But she knew there would be no morning tide. She also knew that the Admiral, although he was always talking about it, would never go to sea again. It was far too far away from land and it always made him seasick.

"Obey the rules! Observe the bye-laws!" The Park Keeper rushed past, blowing his whistle.

"Ship ahoy there! Heave to, old salt!" The Admiral seized the Park Keeper's sleeve. "That's my hat you're wearing, skipper. I won it in a hand-to-hand fight off the coast of Madagascar. Didn't I, Messmate?" he demanded.

"If you say so, dear," murmured Mrs Boom. It was better, she knew, to agree than to argue. But privately she was aware of the facts – that the hat belonged to Binnacle, a retired pirate who kept the Admiral's ship-shaped house as shipshape as only a pirate could; and, moreover, that neither he nor her husband had ever clapped eyes on Madagascar.

"And I thought I had lost my Skull-and-Cross-bones! Where did you find it, you son of a sea-snake?"

"Well, it fell down, sort of, out of the sky." The Park Keeper shuffled uneasily. "And I put it on by mistake, so to say, not meaning any harm, Admiral, sir."

"Nonsense! You're thinking of cannon balls. Pirate hats don't fall from the sky. Hand it over to Mrs Boom. She carries all the heavy things while I spy out the land." The Admiral took out his telescope and fixed it to his eye.

"But what am I going to put on my head?" the Park Keeper demanded.

"Go to sea, my man, and they'll give you a cap. A white thing with H.M.S. Something on it. You can't have my pirate hat, I need it. For away I'm bound to go – oho! – 'cross the wide Missouri."

15

And the Admiral, singing lustily, dragged his wife and the hat away.

The Park Keeper glanced round anxiously. What if the Lord Mayor came along and found him with his head uncovered? He dared not think of the consequences. If only the long day were over. If only all these crowding people, lolling or strolling hand in hand, would go home to their suppers. Then he could lock the Park Gates and slip away into the dark where his lack of a cap would not be noticed. If only the sun would go down!

But the sun still lingered. No one went home. They merely opened paper bags, took out cakes and sandwiches and threw the bags on to the grass.

"You'd think they thought they owned the Park," said the Park Keeper, who thought he owned it himself.

More people streamed in through the Main Gate, two by two, choosing balloons; or two by two from Mudge's Fairground, buying ice cream from the Ice Cream Man, each one holding the other's hand as the falling sun threw their long shadows before them on the lawns.

And then, through the Lane Gate, came another shadow that preceded through the two pillars a small but formal procession – a perambulator packed with toys and children; at one side a girl who

16

carried a basket, at the other a boy in a sailor suit with a string bag swinging from his hand.

Basket and bag were both well stocked as though for some lengthy excursion. And, pushing the perambulator, was an upright figure with bright pink cheeks, bright blue eyes and a turned-up nose – a figure that to the Park Keeper was only too familiar.

"Oh, *no!*" he muttered to himself. "Not at this hour, for Heaven's sake! What's she doing setting out when she ought to be going home?"

He crossed the lawn and accosted the group.

"Late, aren't you?" he enquired, trying, as far as he could, to look friendly. If he had been some kind of dog, his tail would have given a modest wag.

"Late for what?" Mary Poppins demanded, looking right through the Park Keeper as though he were a window.

He quailed visibly. "Well, what I meant to say was – you're sort of upside down, so to speak."

The blue eyes grew a shade bluer. He could see he had offended her.

"Are you accusing me," she enquired, "a well-brought-up respectable person, of standing on my head?"

"No, no, of course not. Not on your head. Not like an acrobat. Nothing like that."

The Park Keeper, thoroughly muddled, was now

18

afraid that he himself was the one that was upside down.

"It's just that it's sort of late in the day, the time when you're usually coming back – tea and bed and that sort of thing. And here you are, sallying forth, as though you were off on a jaunt." He eyed the bulging bag and basket. "With all and sundry, so to speak."

"We are. We're having a supper picnic." Jane pointed to the basket. "There's plenty of everything in here. You never know when a friend will appear – so Mary Poppins says."

"And we're staying up for hours and hours," said Michael, swinging his bag.

"*A supper picnic!*" The Park Keeper winced. He had never heard of such a thing. And was it even permitted, he wondered. His list of bye-laws raced through his head and he promptly gave it tongue.

"Observe the rules!" he warned the group. "All litter to be placed in the proper containers. No eggshells left lying about on the grass."

"Are we cuckoos," demanded Mary Poppins, "to be scattering eggs in every direction?"

"I meant hard-boiled," said the Park Keeper. "There never was a picnic, ever, that didn't have hard-boiled eggs. And where are you going, might I ask?" If the picnic was to be in the Park, he felt he had a right to know.

"We're off to –" Jane began eagerly.

"That will do, Jane," said Mary Poppins. "We will not hob-nob with strangers."

"But I'm no stranger!" The Park Keeper stared. "I'm here every day and Sundays. You know me. I'm the Park Keeper."

"Then why aren't you wearing your hat?" she demanded, giving the perambulator such a forceful push that if the Park Keeper had not jumped backwards, it would have run over his foot.

"Step along, please!" said Mary Poppins. And the little cavalcade stepped along, orderly and purposeful.

The Park Keeper watched till it disappeared, with a swish of Mary Poppins' new sprigged dress, behind the rhododendrons.

"Hob-nob!" he spluttered. "Who does she think she is, I wonder?"

There was no one at hand to answer that question and the Park Keeper dismissed it. Uppity – that's what she was, he thought. And no great bargain to look at either. She could go where she liked for all he cared – the long Walk led to all sorts of places: the Zoo, St Paul's, even the River – it might be any of them. Well, he couldn't patrol the whole of London. His job was to see to the Park. So, ready for any misdemeanour, he cast a vigilant eye about him.

"Hey, you!" he shouted warningly, as the tall man who had washed his face in the fountain bent down to smell a rose – and picked it! "No picking of flowers allowed in the Park. Obey the rules. Remember the bye-laws!"

"I could hardly forget them," the tall man answered. "Considering I was the one who made them."

"Ha, ha! *You* made them! Very funny!" The Park Keeper laughed a mirthless laugh.

"Well, some of them, I admit, are funny. They often make me chuckle. But, have you forgotten, it's Midsummer's Eve? Nobody keeps the bye-laws to-night. And I myself don't *have* to keep them, now or at any time."

"Oh no? And who do you fancy you are then?"

"One doesn't fancy. One just knows. It's the kind of thing one can't forget. I'm the Prime Minister."

The Park Keeper flung back his head and guffawed. "Not in that silly cap, you're not. Prime Ministers wear black shiny hats and white stripes down their trousers."

"Well, I've been having a game of cricket. I know

it's too small. I've grown out of it. But you can't wear a top hat when you're batting – or bowling, for that matter.''

"I see. And now you've had your little game, you're off to visit the King, I suppose?" The Park Keeper was sarcastic.

"Well as a matter of fact, I am. An important letter arrived from the Palace as I was leaving home. Now, where did I put the wretched thing? Drat these skimpy flannel pockets! Not in this one, not in that. Can I have lost it? Ah, now I remember!" He wrenched off the offending cap and took from within it an envelope sealed with a large gold crown.

"DEAR PRIME MINISTER," he read out. "IF YOU HAVE NOTHING BETTER TO DO, PLEASE COME OVER TO DINNER. LOBSTER, TRIFLE, SARDINES ON TOAST. I AM THINKING OF MAKING A FEW NEW LAWS AND WOULD BE SO GLAD OF A CHAT."

"There! What did I tell you? And tonight of all nights! One never gets a moment's peace. I don't mind the chat, that's part of my job. But I can't stand lobster. It upsets my digestion. Oh, well, I'll have to go, I suppose. Bye-laws can always be by-passed, but laws have to be kept. And anyway," he said haughtily, folding his arms and looking impor-

22

tant, "what has it got to do with you? A perfect stranger accosting me and telling me – *me!* – not to pick the roses! That's the Park Keeper's business."

"I-I *am* the Park Keeper," the Park Keeper said, shuddering from head to foot as he stared at the regal letter. He had made a terrible mistake and he trembled to think where it might lead him.

The Prime Minister lifted his monocle, screwed it firmly into his eye and regarded the figure before him.

"*I am shocked!*" he said, sombrely. "Even stupefied. Almost, I might say, speechless. A public servant in a public place failing to array himself in the uniform provided! I don't know when I have been so displeased. And what, pray, have you done with your hat?"

"I-I dropped it in a litter basket."

"A *litter* basket! A receptacle for orange peel! An employee of the County Council who thinks so little of his hat that he throws it into a – well, really! This kind of thing must not go on. It would bring the country to the verge of ruin. I shall speak to the Lord Mayor."

"Oh, please, your Honour, it just happened. A little slip when my mind was elsewhere. I'll go through the litter tomorrow and find it. Not the Lord Mayor, your Worship, *please*! Think of my

23

poor old mother."

"You should have thought of her yourself. Park Keepers are paid to think. To keep their minds here, not elsewhere. And not to let things just happen. However, as it's Midsummer's Eve – only once a year, after all – I will let the matter pass. On condition – " The Prime Minister glanced at his watch. "Dear me, it's far too late for conditions. You'll just have to solve the problem yourself. I must hurry home and change my trousers."

He bent down to pick up his bat. "You a married man?" he enquired, glancing up at the Park Keeper.

"No, my lord, my Prime – er, no."

"Neither am I. A pity, that. Not from my own point of view, of course. But to think that there's someone dreaming of me – putting a bunch of herbs under her pillow – Lad's Love, Lavender, Creeping Jenny – and then not finding me, poor woman. Alas, alas, what a disappointment! Tonight of all nights – you understand."

And he strode off, swinging his bat and his rose, his white trousers riding up from his ankles as though they had shrunk in the wash.

The Park Keeper did *not* understand. Who would be disappointed, and why? What was so special about tonight – except the fact that everyone seemed to be breaking the bye-laws; using the public park

as though it were their own back yard? And who could that be, he asked himself, as a curious figure, walking backwards, feet uncertainly feeling their way, came staggering through the Lane Gate?

It was Ellen from Number Seventeen, Cherry Tree Lane, moving like a sleep-walker, eyes closed, arms outstretched before her, meandering over the newly turfed lawn that he had mown that morning.

The Park Keeper braced himself. He would not stand meekly by while the rules were not only not observed but being illegally flouted. Come what might, this was something he would have to deal with, even without a hat. His eyes fell on a small object lying limply beside the fountain. It was the Prime Minister's cricketing cap, left behind, apparently, when he hurried off to change his trousers. The Park Keeper seized it gratefully. At least, his head would be covered.

"Look where you're going! Be careful, Miss Ellen! Beware of swings and see-saws and such. Steer clear of benches, borders and baskets." He strode towards her shouting his warnings.

Slowly, carefully, sometimes sneezing, Ellen came backing in his direction. Then, just as she was almost upon him, the Policeman, suddenly spying her, neatly inserted himself between them and Ellen landed with a bump against his blue serge jacket.

"Oh!" she cried joyfully, as she turned about and opened her eyes. "I hoped it might be you – and it is! What if I had made a mistake and bumped into the wrong one!"

"What, indeed!" The Policeman beamed. "But you didn't. And I'm the right one, see, and no mistake about it."

"It *is* a mistake to do things like that. You might have knocked someone over or got yourself a broken leg. And then who'd be to blame? Me! No backing allowed in a public park!" the Park Keeper warned her sternly.

"But I have to. It's Midsummer's Eve – atishoo! And if you walk backwards on Midsummer's Eve, after putting a herb or two under your pillow – Marjoram, Sweet Basil, no matter what – you'll back into your own true love as sure as nuts are nuts. Unless it's a gooseberry bush – atishoo! If it is, you have to wait till next year. To try again, I mean."

"Well, I'm no gooseberry bush, am I?" The Policeman took her hand in his. "So you won't have to wait till next year, will you?" He tucked his arm through hers.

"But what if you *never* bump into someone? What if it's *always* a gooseberry bush?" the Park Keeper demanded. It might be an Old Wives' Tale she was telling. But with these, he knew, you had to be careful. Unwise to make a mock of them: they were apt to turn out to be true.

"Oh, it's got to be someone someday – atishoo! There aren't all that many gooseberry bushes. And then there's the cucumber, don't forget!"

"What cucumber?" Was this some further silliness? Were they trying to make a fool of him?

"You don't know *anything*, do you?" said Ellen. "Didn't your grandmother tell you nothing? Mine told it to me and hers told her. And *her* grandmother told it to her, and away and away, right back to Adam."

He had been right, the Park Keeper thought. It *was* an Old Wives' Tale!

"Well, this is what you do," said Ellen. "You rub the juice behind your ears, close your eyes, put out your arms and then start walking backwards. It might be a long time or a short. Atishoo!" She paused to blow her nose. "But at last, if you're lucky, you meet your true love."

She gave the Policeman a blushing glance. "It's witchy," she added, "very witchy. But – you'll see! – it's worth it."

"Nothing like cucumber!" the Policeman grinned. "Luckiest vegetable in the world! Well, you've met yours and I've met mine. So the next thing is to name the day. How about next Thursday?''

He took Ellen firmly by the hand and led her away across the grass, tossing aside, as he did so, a spill of toffee paper.

The Park Keeper sighed as he picked it up and gazed after the lovers.

What was to be his lot, he wondered. The world went strolling past in pairs, two by two, hand in hand. Would such a thing ever happen to him? Had herbs been tucked under someone's pillow in the hope of meeting Frederick Smith, the Park Keeper? Would anyone – Snow White, say, or Cinderella – hide her face in *his* serge jacket?

The sun had now laggardly slipped away, leaving behind the long blue twilight – not day, not night, but something between – the hour that is thronged with fate.

The Prime Minister had disappeared and was even now, very likely, taking his top hat out of its hat box. Everyone else, apparently, was bent on their own affairs, even if those very affairs were ruining the Park. No one, as far as the Park Keeper could see, was looking in his direction.

What if – it was nonsense, of course – but what if he gave the thing a try? It certainly wouldn't do any harm. And it might, oh, it might – ! He crossed his fingers.

29

Straightening the blue flannel cap, the Park Keeper glanced furtively round, slipped a hand into his pocket and brought out the crumbling remains of his lunch – a scrap of cucumber sandwich. Cautiously, stealthily, he rubbed the scrap behind each ear and felt the juice of the cucumber as it trickled down into his collar. He summoned up his determination and drew a long, deep breath.

"Good luck, Fred!" he said to himself. Then he closed his eyes, stretched out his arms in front of him and began to walk slowly backwards. Easy now! Step by step. He gave himself to the twilight.

He seemed to be in another world. The Park he knew had dissolved itself into the darkness behind his eyes. Voices that had been near and lively grew faint and faded away. Distant music was wafted to him by people singing in chorus – old songs he seemed to have known as a boy, dreamy, gentle as lullabies. And somewhere a hurdy-gurdy was playing. Bert, the Matchman, of course!

Tch, tch! NO MUSICIANS OR HAWKERS ALLOWED IN THE PARK! But now the bye-laws would have to wait. He had something else to do.

From the right – or was it the left of him? – came the sound of splashing water. Oh, why wouldn't people look at the notice? NO SWIMMING PERMITTED IN THE LAKE. But perhaps it was just the fish rising,

which was what they did at this hour of the day. You couldn't really blame them for that. Fish, after all, can't read.

On, on. His feet felt the bending grass beneath them and the spreading roots of trees. The scent of dandelions rose to his nose, something like dandelions brushed his boots. Where was he? In the Wild Garden? He could not tell and dared not look. If he opened his eyes, he might break the spell. On, on. Backward, backward. His destiny was leading him.

And now about him were whispering voices, rustlings and stirrings and stifled laughter.

"Hurry, you boys!" urged a man's deep voice that seemed to come from far above him. "We haven't got much time!"

Good Heavens, thought the Park Keeper. Were people actually up in the trees, breaking the branches as well as the bye-laws? Never mind. He had to go on.

"We're coming!" piping voices answered, from the height of the Park Keeper's shoulder. "It's the others who are lagging behind. Come *on*, Foxy! And you, too, Bear! Why must you always be such a slowcoach?"

Foxes? Bears? The Park Keeper trembled. Could it be that the Keeper of the Zoological Gardens, bewitched by this thing called Midsummer's Eve, had left the cages open? Might he himself, at any moment, be confronted with a jungle beast, a tiger burning bright?

"Oh, help!" he cried, leaping aside, as a furry form brushed his ankle. Not a tiger, he thought, too small and fleecy. A rabbit, it must be, a wild rabbit. No rabbits allowed in the public parks. He would set a trap tomorrow.

There were scurryings now all about him and a sudden swoop and clap of wings as an airy shape flew past.

Something that felt like a cherry-stone rapped on his cap and bounced away. It was as though it had been spat out by someone much taller than himself, imagining him – the Park Keeper! – to be a litter basket. He was humming, this someone, as he strode by, a refrain that sounded familiar. Could it, perhaps, be *Pop Goes the Weasel*? If so, it was out of tune.

The humming died away behind him. All was silent. The world was still, his footsteps the only thing that moved.

The Park Keeper felt lost and lonely. His outstretched arms were beginning to ache. His eyes were weary of seeing nothing.

Even so, back and back he went. All things come to an end, he knew. And he would not fail whoever it was who was dreaming her Midsummer dream.

33

M.P.C.T.L.—B

Blindly stumbling, backwards, backwards. And, after hours, it seemed, and miles – was he even still in the Park? – he heard behind him a distant murmur: nothing festive, no great clamour, merely the friendly, sociable chatter of people at one with each other.

The murmur grew louder as he neared it. Somebody laughed. Voices were raised and then lowered. Conversation went back and forth. How beautiful, the Park Keeper thought, was the sound of human gossip! Whoever these people were, he was sure, the longed-for "she" would be among them. At last, at last, his fate was upon him. The time had come when he, Fred Smith, like everybody else in the world, would go hand in hand, two by two.

Nearer and nearer came the voices. How many more backward steps were needed? Three would do it, the Park Keeper thought. He took them slowly. One. Two. Three.

And, suddenly – bump! There she was! His spine sensed the shape of a curving shoulder, slender and warm, and his heart leapt. All he need do now was turn and face her. He swivelled round upon his heel and a firm hand thrust him sideways.

"I'll thank you not to behave like a carthorse. I am not a lamp-post!" said Mary Poppins.

The voice was only too well known and the Park

Keeper, still with his eyes closed, let out a cry of protest.

"Never no luck for me," he wailed. "I might have known it wouldn't work. Here I come, looking for my true love, and I have to bump into a gooseberry bush!"

A cackle of laughter rent the air. "Some gooseberry bush!" jeered another voice he would rather not have heard.

With a groan, the Park Keeper opened his eyes and, as though unwilling to believe what they told him, hurriedly closed them again.

He was in the Herb Garden, he realized, with its marble seats and its paved path round a square of chamomile lawn. There was nothing new in that, of course. He had planned and planted it himself. But now on the sward he had mown so often, among the remains of a recent picnic – egg-shells, cake, sausage rolls – were Mary Poppins and the Banks children, Mrs Corry and her two daughters, and his own mother sitting on one of the seats, smiling her welcoming smile.

Nothing new in all that either. But had he seen – yes, he had indeed – he could not deny his own eyes – a Bear sitting snugly beside the hedge, licking a trumpet of Honeysuckle; a Fox on its hind legs picking the Foxgloves; and a Hare in the Parsley patch!

And, as if all this were not enough, Jane and Michael, wearing wreaths of green, together with two unknown boys, scantily clad and similarly crowned, were plucking armfuls of herbs; a big man, armed with a club and dressed in strips of leather, a studded belt about his waist and a lion-skin round his shoulders, was decking Mary Poppins' ear with a double stem of cherries; and a large bird, perched on a bough above her – this to him was the last straw! – was being regaled by the Bird Woman with a sprig of flowering Fennel!

"Mother, how *could* you?" the Park Keeper cried. "No picking of herbs allowed in the Park. You know the bye-laws and you break them!"

This was the first time she had failed him and he felt he could never forgive her.

"Well, you got to make allowances, lad. He only comes down once a year."

"I'm not *allowed* allowances, Mum! And birds are coming down all the time. They can't make nests up there in the sky. After all, it stands to reason."

"Nothing stands to reason, Fred – not tonight, it doesn't."

She glanced from the bird to the animals.

"Well, isn't it very reasonable to come and get the things you need? *I* would!" said Michael stoutly.

"But how did they get here to get what they need?

Somebody let them out of the Zoo!" The cages *had* been unlocked! The Park Keeper was sure of it.

"No, no. They came down with Castor and Pollux." Jane waved her hand at the two boys, as she plucked a spray of Solomon's Seal and tucked it into her looped-up skirt.

"Castor and Pollux! Get along! They're characters in a story. Lily-white boys turned into stars. Tamed horses, that's what they did. I read it when I was a boy."

"And we came down with Orion," said the boys, speaking as though with a single voice. "We came to get fresh herbs for our horse, and he to pick cherries in the Lane. He always does on Midsummer's Eve."

"Oh, does he indeed?" The Park Keeper smiled a withering smile. "Just descends, like, out of the sky, to steal what belongs to the County Council! What do you take me for, then – an April Fool in the middle of June? Orion's up there, like he always is." He flung up a pointing finger.

"Where?" demanded the big man. "Show me!"

The Park Keeper craned his head backwards, but all he could see was emptiness, a large, vacant, unanswering sky, blue as the bloom on a plum.

"Well, you'll have to wait. It's not dark enough yet. But he'll be there, don't you worry – up there

39

where he belongs."

Mrs Corry let out a cackle of laughter. "Who's worrying?" she shrieked.

"You're right," said the big man with a sigh, as he sat down on a marble seat and laid his club beside him. "Orion will be where he belongs. He can't do otherwise, poor chap." He took a cherry from the hoard in his hand, ate it and spat out the stone. "But not yet – ah, no, not yet. There's still a little time."

"Well, you'd better get off where *you* belong – a circus tent, I wouldn't wonder, with all that fol de rol fancy dress. *And* you!" the Park Keeper waved at the boys. "Tight-rope walkers or I'm a Dutchman!"

"You're a Dutchman then! We're Gallopers!" The boys burst into a peal of laughter.

"One thing or the other, it makes no difference. Leave the leaves and I'll burn them tomorrow. We don't want no ragamuffins here."

"They're not ragamuffins! Oh, can't you see?" Jane was almost in tears.

"But what will Pegasus do?" cried Michael, angrily stamping his foot. "They wanted a meal of Coltsfoot for him. So I gathered it. I don't *want* it burnt!" He hugged the herb-filling string bag to him, determined to defy the bye-laws.

"Pegasus!" scoffed the Park Keeper. "He's another of them taradiddles. You learn about them

when you're at school. *Astronomy for Boys and Girls.*
Constellations, comets and such. But whoever saw
a horse with wings? He's just a bunch of stars, that's
all. And Vulpecula, and Ursa Minor and Lepus –
all that lot."

"What important names." The two boys giggled.
"We call them Foxy and Bear and Hare."

"Call them anything you like. Just get out of here,
the three of you. And take your circus beasts along
or I'll go to the Zoo and find the Keeper and have
them put behind bars."

"If a gooseberry bush may make a remark –"
Mary Poppins broke in. "You did say gooseberry
bush, I believe?" she said with icy politeness.

The Park Keeper quailed before her glance.

"It was just a-a kind of manner of speaking. And
gooseberry bush is no libel, it's just a sort of – er –
spiky shrub. And anyway, put it in a nutshell –"
Why shouldn't he speak his mind, he thought. "It
isn't as though you're the Queen of Sheba."

The big man sprang from the marble seat.

"Who says she's not?" he demanded sternly, and
the lion-skin stiffened on his shoulder, the head
showing its fangs.

The Park Keeper hurriedly took a step backwards.

"Well, no one can say she is, can they? What with

41

turned-up nose and turned-out feet and a knob of hair and –"

"What's wrong with them?" The big man glowered, reaching for the club at his side and looming over the Park Keeper, who hurriedly took another step backwards.

Majestically, a pink and white statue, Mary Poppins inserted herself between them. "If you're looking for the Keeper of the Zoological Gardens, he is not in the Zoo. He is in the Lake."

"In the *Lake*?" The Park Keeper stared at her aghast. "D-drownded?" he whispered, pale as a lily. Oh, alas, alas!

"Paddling. With the Lord Mayor and two Aldermen. Fishing for tiddlers to put in a jam jar."

"J-jam-jar? The Lord Mayor? Oh, no! Oh, no! Not tiddlers. It's against the b-bye-laws. Isn't *anyone* observing the rules?" the Park Keeper cried in despair.

The world, as he knew it, had fallen apart. Where now was the lawful authority that he had always served? To whom could he turn for reassurance? The Policeman? No, he was off with Ellen. The Lord Mayor – oh, horrors! – was in the Lake. The Prime Minister was closeted with the King. And he himself, the Park's Park Keeper, important though he undoubtedly was, must carry the burden alone.

43

"Why should it all depend on me?" He flung his arms wide with the question. "All right, I took off a bit of time, which is owed me, after all. And it wasn't much to ask," he lamented. "Only to find my own true love –"

"Curly Locks, I suppose, or Rapunzel?" Mrs Corry chuckled. "You'll find they're suited, I'm afraid. But I've got a couple of soncy girls – Fannie or Annie, take your pick – and I'll throw in a pound of tea!"

The Park Keeper put the suggestion aside as being beneath his notice.

"To find my true love," he repeated. "And all litter placed in the proper baskets. No stealing of herbs from here, nor cherries from the Lane. No one pretending to be what they're not –" He waved at the intruders. "And everyone keeping the bye-laws."

"If you ask me, that's a lot to ask." The big man looked at him sternly. "True loves don't grow on trees, you know."

"Or gooseberry bushes," Mary Poppins put in.

"And what are cherries for but eating? Herbs, too, if it comes to that." The big man swallowed another cherry, and spat out another stone.

"But you can't just pick them because you want them!" The Park Keeper was scandalized.

"Why else?" enquired the big man, mildly. "If we didn't want them, we wouldn't take them."

"Because you've got to think of others." The Park Keeper, who seldom thought of others himself, was quick to deliver his sermon. "That's why we have the bye-laws, see!"

"Well, we *are* the others, all of us. And so are you, my man."

"Me!" The Park Keeper was indignant. "I'm not somebody else, not me!"

"Of course you are. Everyone's somebody else to someone. And what harm have the wild beasts done? A few green leaves one day in the year! It's true that they're not used to bye-laws. We don't have them up there, thank goodness." The big man nodded at the sky.

"And as for pretending to be what we're not – or what you presume to think we're not – how about yourself? Making all this fuss and pother, meddling in things that don't concern you – isn't it rather presumptuous? You're behaving as though you owned the place. Why not look after your own affairs and leave the Park to the Park Keeper? He seems a sensible sort of chap. I always enjoy looking down at him – mowing the lawns, putting waste paper into containers, faithfully going about his job."

The Park Keeper stared.

45

"But it's *my* job he's going about . I mean that *I'm* going about it. Don't you see? He's me!"

"Who's you?"

"Him. I mean me. *I'm* the Park Keeper."

"Nonsense! I've seen him often enough. A decent young fellow, neat and natty. Wears a peaked hat with P.K. on it, not a silly little blue flannel top-knot."

The Park Keeper clapped his hand to his head. The Prime Minister's cap! He had quite forgotten. Perhaps he should never have worn it.

"Look here," he said, with the fearful calm of one who is near to his wits' end. "I'm the same man, aren't I, whatever my cap?" Surely it was obvious. Had circus people no brains at all?

"Well, *are* you? Only you can give an answer to that. And it's not an easy question. I wonder –" The big man was suddenly thoughtful. "I wonder, would I be the same person without my belt and lion-skin?"

"*And* your club. *And* your faithful dog-star. Don't forget Sirius, Orion!" The two boys laughed and teased him. "Sirius can't come down with us," they explained to Jane and Michael. "He'd be chasing all the cats in the Lane."

"Yes, yes, the fellow has a point. Even so," the big man went on, "I can't believe the Keeper I know,

46

that watchful, conscientious servant, would go walking backwards through the Park, eyes closed, hands outstretched, and bits of crust behind his ears. And on top of that – without a 'By your leave' or 'I beg your pardon' – go bumping into an elegant lady as though she were a lamp-post."

The Park Keeper put his hands to his ears. It was true. They were decked with scraps of sandwich!

"Well," he blustered, "how was I to know she was there? And it wasn't the bread that was important. What I wanted was cucumber."

"A proper Park Keeper doesn't go about bumping. And he knows how to get just what he wants. If cucumber, then why bread? You should be more precise."

"I know what *I* want," said a voice from the hedge. "A little of something sweet."

"Have a finger!" Mrs Corry shrieked, as she broke off one from her left hand and offered it to the Bear. "Don't worry, it will grow again!"

His small eyes widened with surprise. "Barley Sugar!" he exclaimed with delight, and stuffed it into his mouth.

"Nothing for nothing!" said Mrs Corry. "Put a shine on my coat for luck!"

The Bear put his paw upon her collar. "It'll shine, when it's time – just wait!" he said.

"What I want is a pair of gloves. I'm going to a party tonight and I like to look well-dressed." The Fox prinked and pranced beside the Foxgloves, as he tried on flower after flower.

"Parsley!" said the Hare from the Parsley patch.

"For his rheumatism," the big man explained. "It's often cold up there and draughty. And Parsley's good for it."

"Coo-roo, coo-roo," the great Bird crooned as he munched his Fennel.

"I do
Like a herb
Or two,
Don't you?"

The Park Keeper's eyes, as large as soup plates, swivelled in all directions.

Had he seen? Had he heard? A finger turned into Barley Sugar? Animals speaking in human voices? No, of course he hadn't! Yes, he had! Was it a dream? Had he gone mad?

"It's the cucumber!" he cried wildly. "I shouldn't have done it. Not behind the ears. She said it would be witchy. And it is! But whether it's worth it, I'm not sure. Maybe I'm not the Park Keeper. Maybe I *am* somebody else. Everything's head over heels tonight. I don't know nothing, not any more."

And snatching the cricket cap from his head, he flung himself, sobbing, across the lawn and buried his face in his mother's skirt.

She smoothed his ruffled hair with her hand. "Don't take on so vainly, Fred. It'll come right – you'll see."

The big man regarded him broodingly.

"A sprig of Heartsease or Lemon balm – either of them would be soothing. Probably needs a rest from himself, whoever he is, poor chap! I even get tired of being Orion." He sighed and shook his head.

"*We* don't need a rest from ourselves, do we?" Castor and Pollux exchanged a grin.

"Ah, that's because you've got each other. But it's often lonely, away up there."

"I never get tired of being myself. I like being Michael Banks," said Michael. "And so does Mary Poppins. I mean, she likes being Mary Poppins. Don't you, Mary Poppins?"

"Who else would I want to be, pray?" She gave him one of her haughty looks. The very idea was absurd.

"Ah, well, but you're the Great Exception. We can't all be like you, can we?" Orion gave her a sidelong glance and picked out another pair of cherries. "That's for your other ear, my dear."

"I've no complaints," the Bear bumbled. "I like

showing sailors the way home."

"I'm going to be a sailor," said Michael. "Aunt Flossie sent me this suit for my birthday."

"Well, you'll need the star in my tail to guide you. I am always there."

"Not if I have Mary Poppins' compass. I can go right round the world with that. And she can stay here and look after my children."

"Thank you, Michael Banks, I'm sure. If I've nothing better to do than that," she gave a loud, affronted sniff, "I'll be sorry for myself."

"Come to the party, that's something better – me in my beautiful foxgloves and you in your new pink dress." The Fox danced on his hind legs and held up his foxgloved paws. "The handsome Mr Vulpecula, arm in arm with Miss Mary Poppins!"

"Handsome is as handsome does." Mary Poppins, with a toss of her head, tossed aside the invitation.

"There's poison in Foxgloves," said Michael, glibly. "Mary Poppins never let us wear them in case we happen to lick our fingers and then have to go to bed, and be sick."

"Foxes do not lick their paws, nothing so vulgar," said the Fox. "They merely wash them in the evening dew."

"Parsley," said a voice from the Parsley patch, with a coughing, choking sound.

Orion sprang from his marble seat.

"Be careful, Lepus, don't eat it! Spit it out, what-ever it is! Ah, that's better. There's a good Hare!" He fossicked among the curling fronds and held up a shiny circular object. "A half-crown piece, by all that's lucky! And he nearly swallowed it."

The four children clustered about it, gazing greedily at the coin.

"What will you spend it on?" Jane asked.

"How could I spend it? There's nothing to buy. There are no ice cream carts in the sky, no pepper-mint horses, no balloons, not even . . ." he glanced at Mrs Corry, "not even a gingerbread star."

"Well, what *is* up there? Nothing but nothing?" Michael found that hard to believe.

"Just space." Orion shrugged his shoulders. "Though you can't exactly say space is nothing."

"And there's lots of room," said Castor and Pollux. "Pegasus gallops everywhere and we take it in turns to ride him."

Michael felt a twinge of envy. He wished he could ride a horse through the sky.

"Room? Who wants room?" Orion grumbled. "Down here you have no room at all. Everything's close to something else. Houses leaning against each other. Trees and bushes crowding together. Pennies and half-pennies clinking in pockets. Friends and neighbours always at hand. Someone to talk to, someone to listen. Ah, well," he sighed, "each to his fate."

He tossed the silver coin in the air.

"Tails up, and you two can have it." He nodded at Jane and Michael. "Heads, and I keep it myself."

Down came the coin on his outstretched palm. "Heads it is. Hooray!" he cried. "If I can't spend it, at least I can wear it. I like a bit of bric-a-brac."

He pressed the half-crown against his belt in line with the three studs already there. "How does it look? Too flimsy? Too vulgar?"

"Oh, it's lovely!" all four children exclaimed.

"Neat enough," said Mary Poppins. "You'll need to keep it polished."

"Gingerbreadish, I'd say," giggled Mrs Corry. "A souvenir to remember us by."

"Souvenir!" Orion growled. "As if I needed reminding."

"He's right. He doesn't," said Castor and Pollux. "He pines all the year for Midsummer's Eve – this is our one night of magic – and the Park and the cherries and the music."

"Don't you have music up there?" asked Jane.

"Well," said Orion, "the morning stars sing together, of course. Same old plainsong day in and day out. But none of your cheerful, homely things.

Polly Wolly Doodle, Skip to my Lou, Pop Goes the What-you-call-it – all that stuff. Listen! They're singing down by the Lake. Don't tell me, I'll get it in a minute. Ah, yes – *Green Grow the Rushes-O.*" He hummed a line of the song.

"He can't sing in tune," the two boys whispered. "But he doesn't know it and we don't tell him."

"And then there's the music of the spheres, a sort of steady, droning sound. Rather like that spinning thing I saw you with today."

"My humming top! I'll get it," said Jane.

She ran to the perambulator that was like an over-crowded bird's nest, with John and Barbara and Annabel asleep on each other's shoulders.

Jane thrust in her hand and rummaged among them.

"It's not here. Oh, I've lost my top!"

"No, you haven't," said a gloomy voice, as a thin man and a fat woman came hand in hand into the Garden. "It fell out on to the Long Walk and we found it as we came by."

"It's Mr and Mrs Turvy!" cried Michael, as he dashed away to greet them.

"Well, it may be and it may not. You can't be certain of anything. Not today, you can't. You think you're this and you find you're that. You want to hurry, so you crawl like a snail." The thin man gave a doleful sigh.

"Oh, Cousin Arthur," Mary Poppins protested. "It's not your Second Monday, not one of your upside-down days!"

"I'm afraid it is, Mary, my dear. And tonight of all nights, when I want to go looking for my own true love, just like everyone else."

"But you've already found her, Arthur!" Mrs Turvy reminded him.

"So you say, Topsy. And I'd like to believe it. But nothing's sure on the Second Monday."

"You'll be sure tomorrow. Tomorrow's Tuesday."

"And what if tomorrow never comes? It would be just like it to stay away." Mr Turvy was unconvinced. "Well, here's your top and much good may it do you." He turned aside, wiping an eye, as Jane set the coloured top on the path.

"Not yet, not yet!" Orion cried, suddenly cupping his hand to his ear.

From somewhere among the surrounding trees a bird gave a quick enquiring chirp that was followed by a rush of half-notes, not so much song as a series of kisses.

"A nightingale tuning up. Oh, glory!" Orion's face was alight with joy.

"It belongs to Mr Twigley," said Michael. "It's

the only one in the Park.''

"Some people do have all the luck. To own a nightingale! Think of it! Come on, come on, my lovely boy! Spin your old humming top, Jane! He'll out-sing it, be sure.''

The four children fell on the shining toy, shouldering each other aside, arguing and complaining.

"I'll start it! No, you won't, it's mine! Me! Me! Me!'' they all shouted.

"Is this a Herb Garden or a Bear Pit?'' demanded Mary Poppins.

"Certainly not a Bear Pit. Bears are better behaved,'' said the Bear.

"But, Mary Poppins, it's not fair!'' Castor and Pollux protested. "We haven't got a top up there. They might give us a chance.''

"Well, we haven't got a flying horse!'' Jane and Michael were equally indignant.

Mary Poppins folded her arms and favoured them all with her fierce blue glance.

"Hooligans, the lot of you!'' she said. "You haven't got this and you haven't got that. Tops or horses – take what you're given. Nobody has everything.''

And in spite, or perhaps because of her fierceness that embraced them all equally, their anger melted away.

Castor and Pollux sat back on their heels. "Not

even you, Mary Poppins?" they teased her. "With your new pink dress and your daisy hat?"

"And your carpet bag! And your parrot umbrella!" Jane and Michael joined in.

She preened a little at the compliment as she gave her characteristic sniff. "That's as may be," she retorted. "And no affair of yours either. I will start the top myself!"

She stooped to seize the handle, and pumped it briskly up and down.

Slowly the top began to turn and as it turned, it hummed – faintly at first but gradually, as it gathered speed, the sound became one long deep note, filling the Herb Garden with its music, a bee-like humming and drumming.

"A ring! Make a ring!" cried Castor and Pollux. "The Grand Chain, everyone!"

And at once they all came into a circle, formally moving round the top as the earth moves round the sun. Right hand to right hand, left hand to left – the Bear with his sugar-stick in his mouth, the Fox dapper in his Foxgloves, the Hare nib-nibbling a sprig of Parsley.

Round and round. Hand to hand. Mary Poppins and the two Banks children, Mrs Corry, her daughters and the Bird Woman, Mr Turvy dragging his feet, Mrs Turvy dancing.

Round and round. Hand to hand. Orion girt with his lion-skin, Pollux with his tunic full of herbs, and Michael's string bag, bursting with Coltsfoot, slung about Castor's neck.

Round and round, each hand taking the hand of each, and the big Bird flying among them. The top spun and the circle spun round it, and the Park round the circle, the earth round the Park and the darkening sky round the earth.

The Nightingale, now the night was come, came to the full of his song. *Jug, jug, jug, tereu!* it went, over and over, from the elder tree, outsinging the hum of the top. The song would never be done, it seemed, and the top would never stop spinning. The circle of humans and constellations would go on turning for-ever.

But suddenly the bird was silent and the top, with a last musical cry, slowed down and toppled side-ways.

Clang! The tin shape crashed upon the flagstones.

And the Park Keeper sat up with a start.

He rubbed his eyes as though waking from sleep. Where was he? What had been happening? He had hidden himself from the fading day and all its unbearable problems. And now the day had disappeared. It had passed through its long blue twilight hour and had almost become the night.

But that was not all. The Herb Garden he knew so well was now another garden. There, in a ring, were people he knew, the familiar solid and substantial shapes of Mary Poppins and her charges, Mrs Corry and her two large daughters, his Mother in her shabby shawl. But who were the others, the bevy of transparent figures, the creatures that seemed to be made of light – insubstantial luminous boys hand in hand with substantial children; a man in a lion-skin, bright as the sun, bending towards Mary Poppins; a Bear and a Hare, both shimmering, a big Bird lifting wings of light and a sparkling Fox with flowers on his paws?

And suddenly, like a man who has lost, and re-gained, his senses, the Park Keeper understood. He had known those figures when he was a boy, and many more besides. And he had forgotten what he had known, denied it, made it a thing of naught, something to be sneered at! He put his hands up to his eyes to hide the springing tears.

Mary Poppins stooped and picked up the top.

"It's time," she said quietly. "The day is gone. You are needed now elsewhere. Castor, put your wreath on straight. And you, Pollux, fasten your collar. Remember who you are!"

"And who *you* are, Mary Poppins!" they teased her. "With your 'Spit spot and away you go!' As if we could ever forget!" They gathered their loads of greenstuff to them.

"Till next year, Jane and Michael," they cried. "We'll be coming to get more Coltsfoot!"

They flung up shining hands as they spoke and then, like the day, they were gone.

"And another pair of gloves!" said the Fox.

"More Barley Sugar!" the Bear bumbled.

"Parsley!" The one word came from the Hare.

And they, too, disappeared.

> *"Coo-roo, coo-roo,*
> *This is for you!"*

The great Bird swooped to Mary Poppins, stuck a wing feather into her hat and then became air and starlight.

Mary Poppins straightened the glowing feather and glanced up at Orion.

"Do not linger!" she warned him.

> *"Linger longer, Lucy,*
> *Linger longer, Lou,*
> *How I long to linger long,*
> *To linger longa you."*

Orion sang tunelessly, and gave her a rueful glance.

"Don't worry, I'll be where I belong, just as that fellow said. "But – to leave all this –" He flung out his arms, as if to embrace the whole width of the Park. "Oh, well – the law's the law! But it's no easy thing to obey it." He gobbled up his remaining cherries, spat out the stones on the chamomile lawn, and took her hand and kissed it.

"Fare thee well, my fairy fay," he said gruffly. And then, like a candle flame blown out, he was there no longer.

"Next year!" cried Jane and Michael shrilly, to the emptiness he had left.

And at that the Park Keeper leapt to his feet.

"No, *now*!" he cried. "They can have them now – all they want, and more."

In a frenzy he dashed from bed to bed, plucking green branches of every kind and tossing them into the air.

"Take them! I'll let the bye-laws be! Rosemary for Remembrance, Mister. All the fodder you need, lads, for the horse! Foxgloves for Foxy! Sweet savours for the beasts and the Bird."

He flung the herbs wildly towards the sky. And to the surprise of Jane and Michael, not a leaf, not a branch, came down – except a small spray of something that Mary Poppins caught in her hand and tucked into her belt.

"Forgive me, friends! I didn't reckernize you!" the Park Keeper called to the nothingness. "And I didn't reckernize meself, neither. I forgot what I knew when I was a boy. It needed the dark to show things plain. But I know who you are now, all of you. And I know who I am, Orion, sir! Cucumber or no cucumber, I'm the Park Keeper with or without my hat!"

And off he darted among the herbs, gathering, bellowing their names, tossing them into the air.

"St John's Wort! Marigold! Coriander! Cornflower! Dandelion! Marjoram! Rue!"

"Really, Smith, you should be more careful! You might have knocked my eye out."

Mr Banks, entering the Herb Garden, removed a sprig of Marjoram from the brim of his bowler hat. "And of course you are the Park Keeper! Whoever said you weren't?"

The Park Keeper took no notice. On he went, madly tossing and yelling. "Good King Henry! Rampion! Sage! Sweet Cicely! Rocket! Basil!"

Up into the air went leaves and flowers and none of them came down.

Mr Banks stared after him.

"What's he doing, throwing herbs around? A Park Keeper breaking the bye-laws! The poor chap must have lost his wits."

"Or found them!" said the Bird Woman softly.

"Aha! So this is where you are!" Mr Banks turned

and raised his hat. "I missed you as I came by St Paul's. Your birds were making an awful to-do. Don't they ever stop eating? And no one was there to take my tuppence, so now, of course, they're starving. Well, what are all of you doing here?"

He held out his arms to his children. "A Midsummer picnic, I presume. You might have left me a sausage roll." He picked up a discarded piece of pastry and munched it hungrily.

"Are you looking for your own true love?" Jane asked, hugging his arm.

"Of course not. I know where she is. I'm on my way to her now, as it happens. And how are *you*, Mary Poppins?" he asked, glancing at the upright figure as it rocked the perambulator. "You're looking very sprightly tonight, with a spray of forget-me-not in your belt and your cherry earrings and Sunday-best hat. That feather must have cost a pretty penny!"

"Thank you, I'm sure." She tossed her head, and smiled her self-satisfied smile. Compliments were no more than her due and she always accepted them calmly.

He gave her a thoughtful, puzzled glance. "You never get older, Mary Poppins, do you? What's the secret? Tell me!" he teased her.

"Ah, that's because she's eaten Fern seed!" The

Bird Woman eyed him slyly.

"Fern seed? Nonsense! An Old Wives' Tale. 'Eat Fern seed and you'll live for ever', they told me when I was a boy. And I used to come and look for it, here in this very garden."

"I can't imagine you as a boy." Jane measured her height against his waistcoat button.

"I don't see why not." Mr Banks was hurt. "I was a very charming boy – about as high as you are now – in brown velveteen and a white collar and black stockings and button-up boots. 'Fern seed, fern seed, where are you?' I'd say. But of course I never found it. I'm not even sure that it exists." Mr Banks looked sceptical.

"And, what was worse, I lost something – the first half-crown I ever had. Oh, the dreams I dreamed of that half-crown. I was going to buy the world with it. But it must have dropped out of a hole in my pocket."

"That must be the one Orion found. He took it away with him," said Michael. "Just before you came."

"O'Ryan? A friend of Smith's, I suppose! Those Irish fellows have all the luck. He's probably spent it by now, the wretch! If I had turned up earlier, I'd have made him give it back. I can't afford to lose pennies, let alone half-crowns."

65

M.P.C.T.L.—C

Mary Poppins regarded him sagely. "All that's lost is somewhere," she told him.

Mr Banks stared at her. For a moment he seemed quite mystified and then, of a sudden, his face cleared. He flung back his head and laughed.

"Of course! Why didn't I think of that? It couldn't fall out of the universe, could it? Everything has to be somewhere. Even so," he sighed, "it would have been useful. Well, no good crying over spilt milk. I must get on. I'm late already."

A hen-like screech rent the air. "You always were!" a voice cackled. "Late in the morning. Late at night. You'll be late for your funeral, if you don't look out!"

Mr Banks, startled, peered through the dusk and saw, half-hidden by the elder-tree, a little old woman in a black coat that was covered with – could it be? – threepenny bits! And beside her two large, formless shapes that might, or might not, be younger ladies.

It was true. He had to admit it. He *was* in the habit of not being on time. But how did this old person know it? And what right had she, a complete stranger, to meddle in his affairs?

"Well," he began defensively, "I'm a busy man, I'd have you know. Making money to keep my family; often working late at the office – it's hard to wake up in the morning –"

"Early to bed, early to rise, makes a man healthy and wealthy and wise. I said that to Ethelred the Unready. But, of course, he wouldn't listen."

"Ethelred the Unready!" Mr Banks was astonished. "But he was around ten hundred and something!" She's dotty, poor thing, he thought to himself, I must humour her. "And what about Alfred the Great?"he asked. "Was he a friend of yours, too?"

"Ha! He was worse than Ethelred. Promised to watch my cakes, he did. 'No need to move them' I said to him. 'Just keep the fire going – and watch!' And what did he do? Piled up the logs and then forgot. Just sat there, brooding over his kingdom, while my gingerbread stars were cooked to a crisp."

"Gingerbread stars!" Whatever next? Really, Mr Banks told himself, Mary Poppins certainly had a gift for making peculiar friends!

"Well, never mind," he said soothingly. "You've still got the real stars, haven't you? They can't get cooked or move from their places."

He ignored her scream of mocking laughter as he glanced up at the sky.

"Ah, there's the first one! Wish on it, children. And another! They're coming thick and fast. Good Lord, they are so bright tonight!" His voice was soft with rapture.

67

"Star light, star bright," he murmured. "It's as though they were having a party up there. Polaris! Sirius! The Heavenly Twins! And where is – ah, yes, there he is! I can always tell him by his belt with its three great stars in a row. Great Heavens!" He gave a start of surprise. "There are *four* in a row, or my eyesight's failing. Jane! Michael! Can you see it? An extra star beside the others?"

Their eyes followed his pointing finger. And, sure enough, faint and small, there was a something – not, perhaps, to be claimed as a star – and yet, and yet, a something!

They blinked at it, half-afraid to believe but, even so, half-believing.

"I *think* I see it," they both whispered. They did not dare to be sure.

Mr Banks threw his hat into the air. He was beside himself with joy.

"A new star! Clap your hands, world! And I, George Banks, of Number Seventeen Cherry Tree Lane, have been the first to spot it. But let me be calm, yes, calm's the word – let me be cool, composed and placid."

But, far from being any of these, he was feverish with excitement. "I must go at once to the Admiral and ask for the use of his telescope. Verify it. Tell the Astronomer Royal. You'll find your way, won't

you, Mary Poppins? This is important, you understand. Goodnight, Mrs Smith!" He bowed to the
Bird Woman. "And goodnight to you, Madam – er
– hum –"

"Corry," said Mrs Corry, grinning.

Mr Banks, already streaking away, stopped dead
in his tracks.

When had he heard that name before? He stared
at the oddity before him and turned, for some
reason, to Mary Poppins.

The two women were regarding him gravely, silent and motionless as pictured figures in a book,
looking out from the page.

Suddenly, Mr Banks was flooded with a sense of
being somewhere else. And, also, of being someone
else who was, at the same time, himself.

White-collared and velvet-suited, he was standing
tip-toe in button-up boots, his nose just reaching a
glass-topped counter, over which he was handing to
someone he could hardly see, a precious threepenny
bit. The place smelt richly of gingerbread; an an-
cient woman was slyly asking, "What will you do
with the gold paper?" and a voice that seemed to be
his own was saying, "I keep them under my pillow."
"Sensible boy," the old creature croaked, exchang-
ing a nod with someone behind him, someone wearing a straw hat with a flower or two springing from it.

"George, where are you?"

Another and younger voice cried his name. "George! George!"

And the spell was broken.

With a start, Mr Banks returned to the Herb Garden and all familiar things. It had been nothing, he told himself, a moment's madness, a slip of the mind.

"Impossible!" He laughed nervously, as he met Mary Poppins' glance.

"All things are possible," she said, primly.

His eyebrows went up. Was she mocking him?

"Even the impossible?" he asked, mocking her in return.

"Even that," she assured him.

"George!" The calling voice held a note of panic.

"I'm here," he answered. "Safe and sound!" He turned away from the moonstruck moment, the trance, the dream, whatever it was.

"After all," he thought, "it's Midsummer's Eve. One expects to be bewitched."

"Oh, George," cried Mrs Banks, wringing her hands, "the children are off on a supper picnic. And I can't find them. I'm afraid they are lost!"

He strode towards the fluttering shape that was crossing the lawn towards him.

"How could they be lost? They're with Mary Poppins. We can trust her to bring them home. For you're coming with me, my true love. Wonderful news! Guess what it is! I think I've discovered a new star and I want to look at it through a spy-glass. If it's true, I'll be made Star-Gazer-in-Chief and you shall be Queen of the May."

"Don't be silly, George," she giggled. "You and your stars! You're always making fun of me." But she didn't mind him being silly and she liked being called his true love.

"Admiral! Admiral! Wait for us! We want to look through your tel-es-co-pe!"

Mr Banks' voice, a fading echo, came floating back to the Herb Garden. And, at the same moment, the chorus of singers by the Lake came to the end of their song.

"Two, two are the lily-white boys,
A-clothed all in green-o
One is one and all alone
And ever more shall be so!"

"Ever more," the Bird Woman murmured, glancing up at the sky. "Well, I must be getting along. I've a dish of Irish stew on the hob and he'll be hungry when he gets home."

She nodded in the direction of the Park Keeper

who was still tossing up twigs and branches and crying their names to the air.

"Good King Henry! Mistletoe! Lovage! All you want, Sir and lads!"

And none of them came down.

"Come, Arthur," said Mrs Turvy. "It's time we were going home."

"If we *have* a home," grumbled Mr Turvy, still very down in the dumps. "What about fires and earthquakes, Topsy? Anything could have happened."

"Nothing has happened to it – you'll see. Come to tea on Thursday, Mary. Things will be better then." Mrs Turvy led her husband away, guiding him through the shadows.

"Wait for me, Mrs Smith, my dear!" Mrs Corry gave her bird-like shriek. The threepenny bits on her coat were a-twinkle and the spot on her collar where the Bear had touched it now shone like a glowing button. "I have to get my beauty sleep or what will Prince Charming say – tee-hee?" She grinned at her two large daughters.

"Stir your stumps, Fannie and Annie," she said. "Come home and stuff some herbs under your pillows – Sowbread and Cuckoo's Meat might do the trick! – and perhaps I'll get you off my hands. Handsome husbands and ten thousand a year. Shake a

73

leg, you galumphing giraffes! Pull up your socks! Skedaddle!"

She made a curtsey to Mary Poppins who received it with a gracious bow. Then away she went, prancing in her elastic boots between her plodding daughters, with the Bird Woman sailing along beside them, like a full-rigged ship, on the grass.

The Herb Garden, so lately full of light and movement, was still now, a pool of darkness.

"Jane, take your top," said Mary Poppins. "It is time we, too, were going home." And the many-coloured tin planet that had hummed and spun so harmoniously was stowed away with the picnic things, silent and motionless, as Jane swung the basket from her hand.

Michael looked round for his string bag and suddenly remembered.

"I've nothing to carry, Mary Poppins," he complained.

"Carry yourself," she told him briskly, as she turned to the perambulator and gave it a vigorous push. "Step along, please, and best foot forward."

"Which is the best foot, Mary Poppins?"

"The one that's in front, of course!"

"But it's sometimes the left and sometimes the right. They can't both be the best," he protested.

"Michael Banks!" She gave him one of her savage

74

looks. "If you are determined to argle-bargle, you can stay here and do it all by yourself. *We* are going home."

He did, indeed, want to argle-bargle and, if he could, get the better of her. But he knew that she always won in the end. And, anyway, it would be no fun to argue with the empty air since it could not answer back.

He decided he would carry himself. But how did one do that, he wondered. He could do it more easily, he thought, with something in his hand. So he seized on the handle of the perambulator and, to his surprise, became a boy who was carrying himself.

Jane came to the other side so that, with Mary Poppins between, all three were pushing together. They were suddenly glad to feel her nearness in the wide unfamiliar darkness.

For this was no longer their daytime Park, their intimate ordinary playground. They had never before been up so late nor understood that night changes the world and makes the known unknown. The trees that, by daylight, were merely trees – something to shade you from the sun or swing on when the Park Keeper was not looking – were now strange beings with a life of their own, full of secrets never disclosed, holding their breath till you went past.

Camellias, Rhododendrons, Lilacs, that by day were clustering shapes of green, were now nameless creatures full of menace, lying in wait, ready to spring.

The night itself was a whole new country, un-mapped and unexplored, where the only thing that could not be doubted was the steady moving shape between them; flesh and bone under its cotton dress, the well-worn handbag and parrot umbrella aswing from the crook of its arm. They felt it rather than saw it, for they dared not lift their eyes. Nor could they be sure, in this crowding darkness, of the bright-ness they had seen. Or had they really seen it at all? Might they not have dreamed it?

To the right of them a bush moved. It muttered and mumbled to itself. Was it about to pounce?

They huddled closer to the cotton dress.

"It must be somewhere,"the bush was saying. "I had to take it off, I remember, in order to find the letter."

With an effort the children lifted their heads and nervously peered through the dark. They had come, they saw, to the Rose Garden. And the bush, edging forward as if to spring, became, by magic, a man. Ceremoniously clad, in top hat, black jacket and striped trousers, he was crawling about on hands and knees, clearly looking for something.

76

"I've lost my cricket cap," he told them. "Here, by the fountain or under the roses. I don't suppose any of you have seen it?"

"It's in the Herb Garden," said Mary Poppins.

The Prime Minister sat back on his heels. '*In the Herb Garden!* But that's at the other end of the Park! However could it have got there? Cricket caps can't fly. Or maybe –" He glanced around uneasily. "Maybe they can on a night like this. Strange things happen, you know, on Midsummer's Eve." He scrambled to his feet.

"Well, I've just got time," he looked at his watch, "to fetch it and get to the Palace." He doffed his hat to Mary Poppins, stumbled away into the darkness and bumped into a clump of bushes that was stealthily moving towards him.

"Really!" The Prime Minister uttered the exclamation as he hurriedly jumped aside. "You shouldn't go creeping about like that – as though you were tracking tigers or something. It gave me quite a start."

"Hssssst!" hissed a bush. "Where's the Park Keeper?"

"My dear fellow, how should I know? I don't keep Park Keepers in my pocket. Nothing's in its right place tonight. He could be anywhere. Why do you want him?"

The clump shuffled a little nearer and became the Lord Mayor and two Aldermen. Their robes were looped up round their waists and their bare legs shone whitely in the dark.

"That's just it. I *don't* want him. We need to get safely out of the Park without him getting his eyes on these." The Lord Mayor drew back a fold of his cloak and revealed a large glass jam jar.

"Tiddlers! You'll catch it if he finds you. The Lord Mayor breaking his own bye-laws! Ask that lady over there." The Prime Minister nodded at Mary Poppins. "She told me where to find my cap. And I must be off to get it. Goodnight!"

The Lord Mayor turned. "Why, it's you, Miss Poppins. How fortunate!" He glanced around warily and tip-toed over the grass.

"I wonder," he whispered into her ear, "if by any chance you've come across –"

"The Park Keeper?" Mary Poppins enquired.

"Sh! Not so loud. He might hear you."

"No, he won't." She favoured him with a Sphinx-like look. "He's far away at the end of the Park."

Gooseberry bush or no gooseberry bush, she was not going to disclose the fact that the Park Keeper, if only for tonight, was letting bye-laws be.

"Splendid!" The Lord Mayor beckoned the Alder-

men to him. "We can nip off home along the Lane and help ourselves ..." he winked at them, "to a cherry or two as we go!"

"I think you will find they have all been picked," Mary Poppins informed them.

"What – *all*?" The three were scandalized. "Vandalism! We must speak to the King. What can the world be coming to?" They spoke to each other in outraged whispers as they scurried off with the jam jar.

The perambulator creaked on its way. Tall, ghostly shapes loomed up before it and turned into swings as it came nearer. A thick black shadow went past sneezing and then revealed itself as Ellen who, wrapped in the Policeman's jacket, was being escorted home. Another moved out from among the trees and was seen to be a solid mass comprising Miss Lark and the Professor, with the two dogs huddling against them, as though anxious not to be seen.

"Goodnight, all!" chirruped Miss Lark, as she spied the little group. "And *what* a good night!" She waved at the sky. "Did you ever see such a sparkle, Professor?"

The Professor tilted back his head. "Dear me! Someone seems to be setting off fireworks. Can this be the Fifth of November?"

80

"Goodnight," called Jane and Michael shrilly, and looked, for the first time, upwards. They had been so intent on the darkness around them and the changes the night had wrought in the earth, that they had forgotten the sky. But the blaze above them, of stars that bent so bright and near – the party evidently in full swing – that, too, was the work of the night. True, the night had created the frightening shapes but then, as though to make amends, had changed them into familiar figures. And what but the night was bringing them, with each turn of the perambulator's wheel, each best foot, – left or right, – thrust forward, to the place from which they had started?

Ahead of them, beyond the line of cherry trees, lights began to appear – not so bright as the ones above but, for all that, bright enough. It seemed as though each house in the Lane, leaning so closely to the next, had lit itself from its neighbour. There were constellations both below and above, the earth and the sky were next door to each other.

"Now, no more day-dreaming, Professor. We want our supper. So do the dogs." Miss Lark seized the arm of her friend, who was raptly gazing into the darkness.

"My dear Miss Wren, I am *not* day-dreaming. I am looking at a fallen star. See! Over there, on that lady's hat." He swept the newspaper from his head and bowed to Mary Poppins.

Miss Lark put on her lorgnette.

"Nonsense, Professor! Falling stars just fizzle out. They never reach the earth. That's just a common pigeon feather – covered with luminous paint, or something. Magicians use things like that for their tricks."

And she whisked him through the Lane Gate.

"Is that you, Professor?" called Mr Banks, racing full tilt along the Lane, with Mrs Banks at his heels.

The Professor looked uncertain. "I suppose it is. People tell me so. I'm never quite sure myself."

"Well, I've glorious news. I've found a new star!"

"You mean the one on that hat? I've seen it."

"No, no! On the Belt, my dear chap. Up till now it has had just three – a trio of shiners in a row. But, tonight, I've distinctly seen a fourth."

"Miss Partridge says it's just luminous paint."

"Paint? Absurd! You can't put paint on the sky, man! It's there, as large as life – and solid. I've verified it. So has Admiral Boom. We've looked at it through his telescope. And who's Miss Partridge, anyway?"

"Lark!" said Miss Lark. "Do remember, Professor!"

"No, no it's not just a lark! He means it. He's seen

it through a telescope and telescopes don't lie."

"Of course they don't. They reveal the facts. So, we're off to the Planetarium. The news must be spread abroad."

"But, George, the children!" Mrs Banks broke in.

"Don't worry. They're all right, I tell you. Put on a hat and I'll change my tie." Mr Banks was panting with excitement. "Perhaps they'll call it after me. Imagine it! Fame at last! A heavenly body by the name of Banks!"

And the happy astronomer dashed away, dragging Mrs Banks by the hand, to the door of his own house.

"Why Banks, I wonder? I always thought his name was Cooper. And I could have sworn it was hat, not belt. But my memory is not what it was – if, indeed, it was ever what it was." Vague and perplexed, yet still hopeful, the Professor looked round for his fallen star.

But Miss Lark was having no more nonsense. She took her friend firmly by the arm and hurried him off to supper.

The Professor, however, need not have worried. His memory was what it had been. His fallen star, even now, was making its way towards the Lane Gate. The feather glowed among the daisies and its light was reflected in the pairs of cherries that hung below the hat brim.

Jane and Michael looked up at it and then from the feather to the sky. Half-dazzled by the resplendent light, they searched for, and found, what they sought. Ah, there! They needed no telescope to tell them.

Among the celestial ornaments, Orion's Belt gleamed on its unseen wearer – three large stars in a slanting line, and beside them, small, modest, but bright as a glow-worm, a fourth piece of bric-a-brac!

Neither the feather nor the extra star had been there when they set out. Their adventure had, indeed, been true. At last they could believe it. And, meeting Mary Poppins' eyes, they knew that she knew what they knew. All things, indeed, were possible – sky-light upon an earthy hat-brim, earth-light on a skyey girdle.

They craned their necks as they straggled beside her, and gazed at the conflagration. How was the party going, they wondered. Was someone strutting in his new-found sparkle; another boasting of his elegant mittens; the others displaying their treasure-trove? And was there anyone up there to remind them, with a toss of the head, that handsome was as handsome did? No! There was only one such person and she was walking between them.

Behind them, Mr Twigley's bird burst into song

85

again. Before them lay the Lane Gate. And as the perambulator creaked towards it they could see a necklace of shining windows beyond the cherry trees. The front door of Number Seventeen, left open by their excited parents, threw a long light down the garden path, as if to welcome them.

"Mary Poppins," said Jane, as they pushed their way on the last lap of the day's excursion. "What will you do with your earrings?"

"Eat them," said Mary Poppins promptly. "Along with a cup of strong tea and a slice of buttered toast." What else were cherries for, after all?

"And what about my string bag?" Michael hugged her sleeve.

"Kindly do not swing on my arm. I am not a garden gate, Michael!"

"But where is it? Tell me!" he demanded. Was Pegasus, even now, he wondered, munching a meal of Coltsfoot?

Her shoulders went up with their characteristic shrug.

"String bags – pooh! – they're two a penny. Lose one and you can get another."

"Ah! But perhaps it's not lost!" He gave her a darting, sidelong glance. "And neither will you be, Mary Poppins, when you skedaddle off."

She drew herself up, insulted.

"I'll thank you, Michael Banks, to mind your manners. I am not in the habit of skedaddling."

"Oh yes you are, Mary Poppins," said Jane. "One day here and the next day gone, without a word of warning."

"But she's not nowhere, even so. And neither is my string bag," said Michael. "But where? Where, Mary Poppins?" Every place, surely, had a name! "How shall we know how to find you?"

They held their breaths, waiting for an answer. She looked at them for a long time and her blue eyes sparkled with it. They could see it dance on to her tongue, all agog to make its disclosure. And then – it danced away. Whatever the secret was, she would keep it.

"Ah!" she said. And smiled.

"Ah! Ah! Ah! Ah!" repeated the Nightingale from its branch.

And above, from every quarter of the sky, there came an echoing "Ah!" The whole world was ringing with the riddle. But nothing, and nobody, answered it.

They might have known! She would not tell them. If she had never explained before, why should she do so now?

Instead, she gave them her haughty glance.

"I know where you two will be in a minute. And

87

that's into bed, spit spot!"

They laughed. The old phrase made them feel warm and secure. And even if there was no answer, there had been a reply. Earth and sky, like neighbours chatting over a fence, had exchanged the one same word. Nothing was far. All was near. And bed, they now realized, was exactly where they wanted to be, the safest place in the world.

Then Michael made a discovery.

"Well, bed's somewhere!" he exclaimed, surprised at his own cleverness. Plain, ordinary bed was Somewhere. He had never thought of that before! *Everything* had to be somewhere.

"And so will you be, Mary Poppins, with your carpet-bag and parrot umbrella, sniffing and being important!"

He gave her a mischievous, questioning glance, daring her to deny it.

"And well-brought-up and respectable too!" Jane added her teasing to his.

"Impudence!"

She swung her handbag at them, and missed.

For already they were darting away to what was waiting for them.

Wherever she was, she would not be lost. That was answer enough.

"Somewhere! Somewhere! Somewhere!" they cried.

And, leaving the dark Park behind, they ran, laughing, across the Lane, through the gate and up the path and into the lighted house . . .

A. M. G. D.

THE HERBS
IN THE STORY
and their botanical, local and Latin names

SOUTHERNWOOD   Old man, Lad's love   *Artemisia abrotanum*

LAVENDER   *Lavendula vera*

MONEYWORT   Creeping Jenny, Herb twopence
Lysimachia nummularia

SWEET BASIL   *Ocymum basilium*

DANDELION   Dens leonis, Swine's snout   *Taraxacum officinale*

CHAMOMILE   *Anthemis nobilis*

HONEYSUCKLE   Woodbind   *Lonicera caprifolium*

FOXGLOVE   Folk's glove, Fairy thimbles   *Digitalis purpurea*

PARSLEY   *Petroselinum crispum*

FENNEL   *Foeniculum vulgare*

SOLOMON'S SEAL   Lady's seals   *Polygonatum multiflorum*

COLTSFOOT   Ass's foot, Coughwort   *Tussilago farfara*

GOOSEBERRY   Feverberry, Goosegogs   *Ribes grossularia*

RAMPION   *Campanula rapunculus*

CUCUMBER   Cowcumber   *Cucumis sativa*

HEARTSEASE   Love in idleness, Herb constancy   *Viola tricolor*

LEMON BALM   Herb livelong   *Melissa officinalis*

ELDER   Pipe tree, Black elder   *Sambucus nigra*

ROSEMARY   Polar plant, Compass-weed   *Rosmarinus officinalis*

FORGET-ME-NOT   *Myosotis symphytifolia*

ST JOHN'S WORT   All heal   *Hypericum perforatum*

MARIGOLD   Ruddes, Mary Gowles, Oculis Christi
Calendular officinalis

CORIANDER   *Coriandrum sativum*

CORNFLOWER   Bluebow, Bluebottle, Hurtsickle   *Centaurea cyanis*

MARJORAM   Knotted Margery   *Origanum marjorana*

RUE   Herb of grace, Herbygrass   *Ruta graveolens*

GOOD KING HENRY   Goosefoot, Fat hen   *Chenopodium Bonus Henricus*

SWEET CICELY   Chervil, Sweet fern   *Myrrhis odorata*

ROCKET   Dame's violet, Vesper flower   *Hesperis matronalis*

BRACKEN   Brake fern, Female fern   *Pteris aquilana*

MISTLETOE   Birdlime mistletoe, Herbe de la Croix   *Viscum album*

LOVAGE   *Levisticum officinalis*

CYCLAMEN   Sowbread   *Cyclamen hederaefolium*

SORREL   Cuckoo's meat, Sour suds   *Rumex acetosa*

COMMON
RUE